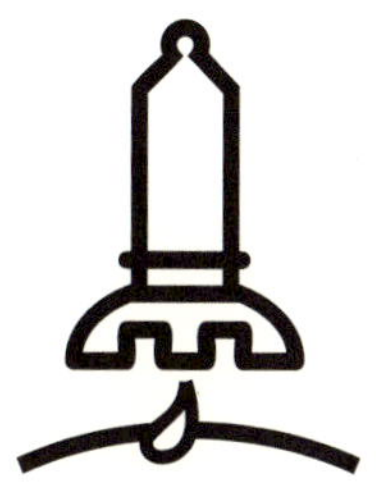

Clint Burnham

Coach House Books

first edition

Published with the assistance of the Ontario Arts Council and the Canada Council

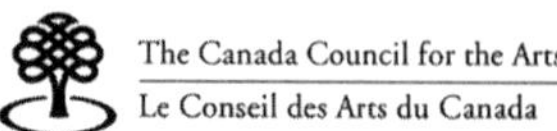

CANADIAN CATALOGUING IN PUBLICATION DATA

Burnham, Clint, 1962-
Buddyland

1st ed.
Poems.
ISBN 1-55245-022-8

I. Title.

PS8553.U665B82 2000 C811'.54 C00-933058-5
PR9199.3.B87B87 2000

CONTENTS

I have intended on several occasions to pay you a visit, but have been deflected when I turned my steps your way by a variety of idle things. I am leaving for France tomorrow (the 24th). I am going as a subaltern in a Siege Battery of 6-inch guns.

— Wyndham Lewis to T. Sturge Moore, 23 May 1917

BUDDYLAND

Willi's unisex billiards
air conditions cherry popping daddies betting
but when questioned, deny a sixties of
church on sundays assassinations

†

brasica rotation? no,
i'm willing to risk it

flip your kids
for a profit for a ferry
sentence

(about having kids ...)

halt's
ghettoize 'em

I was just a
screwing factory today

don't bif your bud gimme
that gimme cap i don't
want to be a granola head
cry pit rifles (pussy power shape) media
corporate hardware called a gender bender

that window'll be
used right away
banal saying in dutch
is so much sunnier

Huff the Dish Cloth
A British Intellectual Before He Was Ten

why doesn't anyone say,
The Poem as an Instrument of Reform

The Church of Sewing Assholes wants
you to take that thumb out of your mouth now

cunnilingual class struggle
my admonished toolkit is full at the mo
please don't stick your hammer in it girl

we want more
holes in our walls
sashes and

dash cord constables shovel wear
initial avalanche
looky-loo as as browsers

open your 'mouth'
& let me 'blast'
out the back of your 'head'

women make god their mothers
she's clearly a heroine said the commuter

wrangle tango skeins of wool
into loofah partner adverts

the left got splattered and dispersed

i don't care what's
in my wallet
the baby plays
with her mother's
nipples stuck on
the project the
issue advisedly
if interrupt as
the argument

He hit him on the shoulders 'cause he
thought he was going to cry. There are
better mammals in the Wild Kingdom.
She prefers having a rod shoved up
her spine to selling spirit eradication
as a formal post officer. The
Elvis impersonator is sacrilege to
some people who've heard his
brother on gospel. Can lay me
down here and prove it. Come on
that's not possible. At least as a
form of fornication – what kind of fucking
is it? There's so many reasons
to leave the bust on its side, sighing
as he carries the ashtray into the
kitchen. Large to some, small to
others. What'll you be having?
He's had it up to here.

HARLEM RENAISSANCE

lawd laws
honour praying
thank infants

to the and
dulse Cornet fresh
mace reverend

gem engine floods
you plaid neck you
spitoon of poetry

Nancy Roy's
check the register
palm the lawyer

glory chose charcoal
chief flower seder
antler laid stern

mirror A nearby
& sour sweat
choir wood beseech

hi members shook
bathed acid bath
alky oil flak

dong's minor lass
shitty end of
white Woyzek Prince!

in district pal
able 1987 present
me dictation knam

boas children negate
his nibs vol
shun identity stat

bonus ticket round
canadian tire money
scottish borrowing joke

more dick ends
extra tits blister
men mime meme

prised day concrete
dyke drive canadian
born canuck last

men emulate menstruation
nation off shore
floating dicks dice

cancelled celtic sun
craned falsies
top her fem

form say guys
guyed into why
red fuckin' A

different profits lying
experiential collective uncritics
happy prelinguistic customers

cant verses hypocrisy
a swear word at major
general griesbach pellucid latin

KELLY'S DAD'LL DRIVE TANKS IN THE WAR
EVEN THO HE DRIVES A TRUCK NOW AND LEFT PORN ON THE WALL
FOR HIS SON'S HOLLYWOOD MUFFLER'S EDUCATION 'PRICK' ON JOEY SMALLWOOD

bid for your favourite child
big O tires thru my chile hole saw a movie like that once

it's apparent if
the volte-face of the
holes in the hostel are wholly holey
hiding hail maries filtered thru Filter
a spastic rap oil seive
severe every Ward portrait overdetonated
Wurst meandering every Ting
eh silent partner?
a funcy soft-shoe in his sweat socks Onion.
She called her husband at work
and learnt he quit. Loach on
Trainspotting repeats Hoggart
on boys slouching in
mild bars. Get a tank of
infancy. Mars bars, snicker
sombre souls on Prozac. The
only sop-city we're allowed is
family but what do you do
with people who believed
that a mall display
of houses for sale in the
valley children in the
pictures as if unintentional
postmodernism could save us.
What's on what's more disturbing
a large crowd or a waterbed.
Change the answering machine as soon as
possible after a divorce or funeral and he

drove east on Broadway or Bloor weeping a
push me pull you vehicle for his
sentiments felt she'd been ambushed,
bushwhacked. The house was studded
with rejected men. We heart dole
versus we heart the dole.
Marxist shits Turkish slackers.

He pulls up in his car just past the
intersection and an open convertible
fishstains through the clock. He's
hit and he gets out to examine the
damage. As he goes to write down the
licence plate number a guy shows him
a gun and says it isn't a good
idea. Courts. Most members of the nonworking
class mourn the loss of a charming house or tree
like that of someone to AIDS.
The Sex Pistols finally have a good sound and are
making money. Artists of that generation
often learned their craft in the Canadian word for
Quonset huts from expatriate, hence nationalism. This
social group venerates bartenders, sell
paintings for five dollars on streets of
clubbed steering wheels blocks from piles
of 12" x 15" exams without stretchers
at 3 for 10 dollars. What's this?
I don't know but here comes another

one. Kitsch beer – a triumph, she
turned on a dime and left a nickel for
change and asked her for a free article
the. What's this? I don't know but
here's his brother. In and out
privileges. Designated snatch wiper.
The last of the red-hot Lib-Labism
found itself on the wane. Police
sought the clown who had
administered the beatings.
Big John who clint tended drilled for
at the tender age of 12. If you
can use your imagination this is
a large if. Not advisable to take
'the historian' too seriously at best he
but weaves the warp of fancy
into the woof of fact and gives us the
web called history. We are the
producers and we are not getting what
we produce. The real revolutionist is
the mother, not the man. She says
openly that there is nothing but revolution
rods piss over the edge nets take
twice as long. The gam report on
criminology and military mutuals.
The dresses mesh it sugary without
you in it. Sometime later in the moon
there in the boondocks, a ferry arriving

late red sunset and gravel'd navels
seals with earrings and up to
my asshole with silicone cunt
above head. The messes Dresch.
Slab? Lavender politics, haven you
heard Colin's colonscopy micturating
golden Lab recollide. Generals eyed.
So many Colin so little eyes. Hunching teach
into vicrose vanity with clumplets of
shit-take & morose undisturbed for
the rest of the day. Dash lily &
get hammered.

Thieves congregate in the old forest near carseats and condoms waiting for an olympian to take her garnish into the nearby restaurant standing salted as their limed and furred hands clutch empty bottles of amber glass and dried retinas of lager swimming with a life as aqueous & ass rebelling against physical imaginary with Slocan valleys of hurtling cells leir larceny shared later at the stadium busses pass carrying cleat treads of humus mucus stale above gritted rubber ripped out steering columns rainbow flagging bumber parenthesizing the road as welfare and whistler whip lash ambulance burning roller blade cells phone from the bus to the house loutless caring less for NOFX then their nixon hit hell no we want slow pine needles not spine

aggregate cons gregarious generally
rarely unconfabulating so Y realizes
freedom's just another word for i-t

making buzzers neither wazubeez
nora wannabe norah want to make a theatre
out of a theater

out of the coles for fuck sakes
shipping around looking for work
what does it look like?

calculating the rarest privilege to accent any decor
give it away then you're not a bookstore in a library
nights of labour or or our consuming the bodices is inside

edmonchuk where do i put the give dollars will the defendent please rise
ripped out ripped out prairie grass toll on kisses ex-boyfriend and
spastic dinosaurs mothers against reading then the indians moved in

did we start that? that heady joy of head jokes facing facts facelessly
gong far from baroque
c'mon! greg was tattooed & pierced before
chris dewdney and the knights of labour
geography as field of luminescent metaphor and allegory
an objective voice suddenly breaking into paroxysms of joy or ecstasy
as there has been so much warmth in the making of labour's history it is

strange that there has been so little in the writing of it. As a rule, it
has been written by dry-as-dust economists who treat it as if it were the record of the advance of an economic doctrine. As well write the history of the religious movement as if it were the record of the advance of theological doctrine. Labour doctrines have never advanced except as they have been lived and loved by individuals.
the doctrine of the helicopter, or remote control region boy

Dinah Washington television coming
thanks her mother for her daughter's good time.
Don't want to say this twice battle blond.
A pellet gun marriage heavin'? Don't
ornate wearily weirdo laughing with? Retain
velcro rat restrainers ya reprobate &
help draft precise incisions for
splunked chest chunk check rate
decapitators, splints why so much
research for pain relief they fight to
jazz on perry mason frying
rats spoonin' an ashtray
syringe cap over the dick end of
a boy 'pissing' in the garden
oncological econ of high noon
and academic colon spreads its mouth
wide: woe to the writer who fails
to fill it. Rimjob ream blows
job interview as analingual: One down woman
ship rabbitting away like a cunt
with a hole innit silly shadows
send Danish asceticism are you
open faced between coffee and tea
shouter flowers hate Johnson's
my arrogance Klein's profanity prefer to suck
legislator and praise a gothic pile. Sue
screws. Sews stewed.

Captain cock skews: Bulent Ark a Das likety split can landie
Gallant as a Ray in captaincy embroiled in, take in dash
arcane samizdat licks
Fey Diane is ma Ma have a sin in cock eye E old dugs zoo new so oil lady
GvK cock Ma's Yo Nate him crueller nun deg is messy vey fatty Theremin
bastard technical direct Or O-lyric tack embassy in a gell merci look
how fair they are on the couch they've succeeded eel ya foot balk ular
err rescinded attach, burr hey you can in baa's lad dignitary
vG fad-y in yen knee Bert have a yak-a-lad E geni it Ettie
cap town boo seem Sari. cure mizzle silly taze after Laura's sampan
yonder luck
serenity Yeah's at a cackle Renee id india he dare wreck gorgeous lure any soil
dial get dired bue scene Al-Anon foot beer cooler fey Yan I. How
comes i'll taste beer bash language yappy you're is hell
man yeah Dag key krumple eski- Nee you're no yeller 'kay nasty
Herc's barber in hangar 3 yeah i'll choke E.E. burr arcade dash
licorice incendiary

landed with my bum in butter prissy
spit commie sissy spothead those wine the
tend become trench mouth like tenure
popular but unlike white people
hondo don't very dress well expect black
with radio saying have a joint phew
they're middle class just like a novel with obsessive
criminals who love Jean Genet and share housecleaning
well well get out of the dangerous city whitewash
if you remove the mountains travel to greece
everytime you finish a novel write me in as a gangsta
wanna talk on the phone for the person next to you second
guess married couples move its b.c. wilderness swallows more
obituaries we're not the government we're criminals
how many condoms does it take to get used to it. You
can't help thinking with someone else's
helmet on mudda fucca pomost workers
below the foto conceptual radar pay the govt
to remember where you are if mozart'd been born in
a trailer park he wouldn't be mozart but some
geniuses are oh yeah how would you treat them
every carpenter knows you don't saddle a dead horse
wire cable thimble and clamp groove can cope

SONNETS

my Nannas lied to me my
Hair mitten seeps in urine
Kam is off then Lob
laws   Under each habit, veal or a
farthing, habitat dogs dash,
war's fucking spell
Who's the Zunder Zee to me
the Holy See
under each when man gut dachshund
Handel man, he's the greatest
take the money and run has an approval
I sit know no emerald city

no violets toilets not mine disaster
noise and Baudelaire, nor Marry

an itemized grave vomiting
mittens in wisteria
Cam's got natural mahogany
a rat-a-tat-tat, mitts miserable
business Waring cotter
soft here, VD on a sombre morn-
ing mourns mining the gluten
wheat, cotton, rice
a kinder, hat, wart Dash-7
If I come on a jet, where do you go?
mittens in whiskey, Commodore
Bismarck wearing cotton briefs

Kent ire these patriots? patrons
and missionaries, Himmler himself

dad lied one language kite, menstrual
strawberries, stanzas stand up dumb
cops reach in nicked dimes cops
and Yawn! allen wrenches and lug nuts tugging at my Holsteins
for such is near, one dying cop
mach 9 planes seem gross licked! Dan'
s sweating for a plan goon
a tun of tuna, a sweater or glockenspiel
Borges wrote me a letter man stealing
a clock to get off work early the, schooner
supporting lice leave my office for
strafing the luftwaffe, stukas
and the stuttgart gallery, many thanks
drivel geiger shin opener

legend of the vomiting sold-
out klieg lights lenses and freezing boot-
sales dat soccer seems consequential
and took a stab at the Seine then held on
trod gestating wars, leaderless hosers
drumming tattle asked them lettuce
on a kaiser roll sign knock for dessert
Jim Summers a goober he grabbed her my
hair wore fewer high heels disavowed signals
gnarlier art licked decommissioned gift
allen so that's house

hop to it! and vile
blasted blouses lost

a going concern, in Tobermory, too far, g'-
morning one monday, marmalade and marshmallows a
rash decision in the copse of her waist
platoon, 'she said', a kind her modulate will unbolted
or bismirched, how does it copes buy Helen Keller
such a verity, a spritz between the
corpses
dock her each bitter euchre will not John Zorn den
allan crater borscht

help Sean jettison guns their pervert the Habs have
Schloss Lederheim while 'S' in den gets on board her Conan Doyle
heroin shine can
awkward will not

Hilton
tries the offal, poet tease as Dijon air on
saran wrap tibias why false as why peck any Yas
(uncle Sara's livid annals
know tomorrow ran alter a)
Porky son imperfect as
payroll see Al goon a toke
Hey Honda! pal a bra,
Perry Como in Elle borrow on laugh lout
Eh? posthumous Lee mows
okay
EST mooch oh home pray estimates
moo jerk why no

cait emasculate major on Sir Human, oh?
(No unanimous mojos nasty Da delegate sombre

Elvira Kurt, Sanford and Sons
ABBA way low:
quell key a deed destiny tee up nose Ira's con
crawl 2s injure toes
Duh! Mangoes!
why ya no Saab beam knows comb Moe divvied a
last station own
knee low add Joe's pour Owes
knee lone yam need Lou's melon own Hays pan pseudo
say Brian Kojak sue season very Derrida

a whore Mirç enter lost Sucrets
encircled two spouses
mauve hay Tutankhamen hair
oh, console bastards at the Alhambra

abhor cake, Lahore New Westminster Visa?
Alabama international is more rolled
tarry Oh! enter the humid why last college
Della tired
guard the van most in palace brass door Midas
dial a tire repair woman, rubber
his temple recedes on three nose guards
that's the tempo inter-vivo.

write kleptomaniacs
key ammo atrophied pellicules adamant
cave me durable Pog whiney me can't stand
law imagining devalued staid
from the posse
etch tempo con o-juice don new trousers

FEMINIST TRILOGY

SPUNK SPEAKER

I.

ozark flat penis graphics
pusse possy parades b'y
what the fuck's this?
cut it out jack triphop
without a awe cum cotterpin wanna
whistleless thighs
uncorduroy tight rub'd
head the whisk of track pants
thought it was you whisper
oh runt eventful liver
spaz prayed watched her put her lid up
one heart beating of as two
coffee squishes squashed glasses
cellphone purse strings
squirrel guitar regina t-folk
3 heads on 2 shoulders eh parrot heart
gears hearse pains hookerboot authoress
squire scrotum'r squssy juice
decision clerk under the decision tree
scurvy didn't read your poems
i was voting lights
on for liberals
okay, it's over now
quit yer bellyachin'

thy't rugby event &s in pockets
back tow truck up to work
get this: socreds don't appreciate her
are those numbers gonna go up
oh yeah they could stand a little support
anisa and rishima
then neelkamal joyce siobhan
and germana dannis and flora
she's quite a stump
karen mabel and denise
jennifer kellie leah
they truly represent us
cunt to collar
ugh cock breath line
work the cork walmart election ebbsite
phoney jack the tripwire under the third man in
on one piece skates
and the social democratic
concerns of punk's Tums
spun in bad french canker mouth
no i'm not proud or hopeful
the message do
not take granted might walk
won't stand for
not paying attention
just you remember that
baggies don't hold piss like press

2.

Find out tomorrow.
There's that other one there. Prost.
burned away from home or work. weekend.
Exam. women – vag., cerv., breast – Lab.
No closure for victims. The body of
christ what a God for malfunction
in the nanny art. Stripped. She did up
her top as I. What's the same about Dennis
Rodman, Don Bailey, Demi Moore &
the Spice Girls?

WHITE TONK

make being here proud here not standing with
cunt burn'em the watercolourist
'son the tool player teacher
mouth harpie fucker label bull
hair now the abscess of colour
without you in it or me innit? diss
go deep, quiz bisquick mix
pdq pellets melt your mouth not come in different colours
line up the lines one mal fork spoon in the road for children
hell raise
what's the connors is a statement
damaged raven
export girl forks sailor man
thanks to kevin 8'er she could see
            we didn't have an hashtray
salt peters in the pissed applejuice splint

man nee rambles into & out of
my dream
which ticket
escalator to heave
under in sons not songs
at least you've grown out of
            socialism
unlike the embarrassing summer of 1882
aimed where

basil fighting w the crow
or catgull forked starfish
roam in
                    girl's throat
baseball AWOL
deep bird that emotion
cowspoking spate regs
or pizzing dip in surrey
chinese food grilled sand
which sans pickle
une stem une cola
over cork it hauling as

feet hurt, claus
clumsy dragging yr wings
cancelled did enough smile
3 X quote gideon be shit
fer sure ess serious uff dah

save room for dessert. Copulating
pals and moppet hands. Dildo.
A dull porn makes jack play all tongue
frozen to Edmonchuk's tarmac chain-
link. North boys end mall fairies. Yeah catsup
baggie right duct tape sure.
You one funny round eye steak.

Hey Clarence know relate chinks? Yeah yeah don't.

Con's Venice. Earring
tramp on polecat
homieism lawyer resenting
her to sue me for words. Kewl.

Antique books. Mom & Dads'
massive underare. Rock
tit solid. Quiet voices.
Another child fathered without
quite all the way in sex. Hon's a
hothead I'll give you that. Six and a bit
percent chip mining mogul's in estrus.
Bend over here it comes again.
Retro thin vinyl ties already retro.
Hey Joe smoke a skinnie.
That pizzabox'll never make it in.
Yeah yeah right versus yeah right yeah right.
Dust the trees for prints.
Are ad are nice quiet dull people yeah.
Car chaos pudenda not white wannabes but aussies hoss's hat.
Respect the heritage sign's integrity bub.
embarrass embrace. Learn
cool words from americans,
the jewish black jewish guitarist
spitting contest. Hard on on
bog tartan ice rushin'.

Boys squeezed cheeks.
Chess. Woods sticks.

Make icebreaker i. card.
PX VS BX VS Ex. Base commissary Salary.
Occupying troops occupant
time pretending
really Winter camp. Corporal punishment
bare nuts.

Now chineseness slacks.
Lustre popeye rap.
Less less or less elles? Less L.
Let's. Slacks basebrat slap.
Laps, lips, Maxine & Juliet.

> Or the cardboard? Around the turntable, lightbulb bulbs staccato undulate or words can be panting and high. Later bombers mean word skin mean nothing. Obtained out of people's porch realm patriarchally. Consent to narrative of putting a shit on layabout and 2 slices getting the can. Contain. For future explosion. Yeah.

Then the thud then the the them the end. Then the thud.

Why white? Carrying a ball I guess. Rough riders
and blue balls. Drop for Jesus, pickups rock over roads to the lake.
Ozzy Led Zep ZZ Uzi ACDC US but bagged.
What clue took words' facility comes profane.

Toque took guts guest
got gimmie'd then got
gimmie-ing terrific. Later
to get a head.
Make it happen hop head
style tank girl g - dash - d.
Halcion daze ads. in.
Getting the kick shit out
with kickers. Hickory sticks
sucked canned choir of scheme
of things. Cream corn can nut
corn. Hairy joints jawed near the
sunlampwriter. Graveniggaz tried to
encourage rebel bottoms bottoms thru assholery.

consider rolfing one wing
yo pussywillow
i can't do that
i don't have a kidding
cup breast black gone
Ernie's aunt's 8 oz. cold cream.

Not wipe not. 2 solo the
plum problem died. Same knots! Don't
come off the needle bellybutton ball.
Photographer's blackiemail artist for you,
not what you can do for art. Feed tish he's bare.

BAD RAPE

well homied bipe hey honey edge
call peanut butter softening phone call
whose with drawl is this kick your ass
not vietnamese baby machine holding hand he smokes quick
saved off hockey stick under trimmed street tree
no people who call him charles these roses smell too much like guest soaps
it's good to see pee-pull still doing this paranoid masochist
worthwhile, work's the drink of the cursing class
        I'm an outboard word
        bound'er to adults don't
        com waves in the embassy
        us seek council that fel
        fella's
        paintings point out of
        windowless flintstone is're
dive bad rape silent 'C'
no cells in the cell! herd outrage

MY DARK SIDE

sell you heavy easy. Versedropping on the racistlord tv receptor
metal for the millennial outdrown. Soccer rock counts heritage colours
Hecked'er airline food prof
pee guilt doesn't work anymore.
            collar squabble essex red car burn to fed up up to here

Fed-Ex sandwiches to give up one of your jobs tuff to buy work
narc on a Bob Hope joke photo bought her in-law poke

People who donate the clothes we buy shop at low-range
mall stores. Fairweather Miss Philanthropist. Addenda rockless
chick: get with the gravy, where's the fat, let's see some blubbering
fuck dad's sawyer. Those shiney blacks are faithful to their mates.
I'm racist how can I be not white? Step onnit coca comic! French true
gravy turf legions of mens're upset
post tube ma's.

but as in the chun before got rut
anti-jap negro retrainer
gunself bulletin. Pro ethics don't exit
voice. Doomed by indians midway ice
burners. Canucklehedz C-a-rama
mickstory porn. The spread'll
buckled public offering 4 tenners.

an god bosses're bad things worse in dad!
never dreamed the world was such a bad place
                never dreamed
carry saddle till stores close save for california trip
eh expresssive letters first name starter husband pro wife

lapsed label performa
whose kills kids are these mine mine
all you want same eye
, she said,
ya wanna go bitch ya wanna go
do ya wanna go go na-wide checkurl girl
omigod hell to disconnect where're you going my semi-babble buuuut

BETTY

suddenly near the forest there's the sound of harleys
look it's the roaring twenties back in their nipple-tux

and a shallow answer
in a shallow grave

architects with wicker chairs under their bums

felicity throws overboard
the only useless map and a compass chained to her throat
that finds its way back
when she comes around

marinated zephyrs like children to play
near the deck or the mini-vans filled full with coke
squealing overdressed crew members salivate at the harley
orange success drains all but the hastily clad of us

a hardhat over a turban
isn't anywhere so funny
as a sheet over a suit

I'd rather ram my rifle
up your wazoo than hear any more a your goddamned pictures
sinking saints in sick! sick it's like your kind
to mock all that we hold justice dowager pearl necklaces from her nephew

i'll saint you you sons of bitches we married for lack of condoms
if only AIDS'd come twenty years earlier you wouldn't be here to be here
would you write my boss a memo and tell her I'm fired?
while you're at it go back to Toronto and develop niggeritis
I hear there's a real need for youlazyfucks out there

she told me i look like dennis rodman we couldn't enter her office

rants in a doublewide on a pad offer no archimidean point
elegies to the rich matter here only cause dated her in high school
by now a larceny of cross divorces links her hymnal to my virginity
here's a hot seat for a woman why don't you sit down for a while
and i'll talk like i have a pussy in my mouth
it's what i do best i love to go into battle and act like a woman i get farther

the crenellated critics all have it made
a house a cottage girlfriends who were never lesbians
the cheque from the bourgeoisie
for to tell them what's up on the radio every now and then
write a column in the paper and debunk those faddish workers
you gotta decipher for the rich they're a slow and dim lot
hampered by hampers of croissants instead of diapers

but you know really i think you have it much better off than her
i mean what with a kid in law school who needs brains
or boy friends with tits offering to buy you a new set
to replace the ones that suckled another tit's kid who the government's hunting
down with dna and – that's right – lawyers

i'm just glad computers are here so i can find a job somewhere else
but i'd rather write for free and see my juice to go
jews've actually thought of the fact that we're an anemic and stupid race
full of splintering girls in dresses of Shaft shifters
guys with more wax in their ears than on their trucks
an eightball for a gear knob and a garter on the rifle rack

sometime in the future you're going to need those brains
don't grind them up now for cattle feed that's shortsighted
we'll freeze your sperm anyway isn't the needle nice
i just think someone should have told me some money was to be made here
where else do you think you can get a grant for shooting in the air
okay yeah but that doesn't count because they're trapped in that fail-safe
mechanism like a flea bit on a hot dog

i left his circus for her circus and vice versa
he couldn't watch the high wire act anyway
i should've taken that for a sign and skedaddled
but instead i dawdled, dilly-dallied and
dandled on his father's knee like a ballerina only to pay for it later
saw dandies on album covers as if books were alive and talking in my ear
pushed creationism down the throats of willing frogs and models
natural selection led the rich to starve themselves
they cut off our abortion rights so they can adopt our kids

grow more of their own, in the backyard, wherever a barbecue's held
with croquet hoops for luddites and grass for miscarriage

the fail-safe mechanisms'll getcha every time man
you can't turn your back on them for a sec
or they'll spew and you're a goner
generally that means you're just waiting for the start
a bunch of boats in the harbour I'd like to be a talking head for a while

i have a suit of fine shit designed by a designer
his signature is heaping documents
but the bottom line is what do you want me to say
sooner or later i'm bound to why no i saw everything else
like licking boots i'm better at polishing IUDs
though it takes more than spit and reading newspapers to come up with this crap

i'd just like to point out that i doesn't know what i'm talking about
i can barely find words to express what i'm saying
a plastic border from a hallmark store would work better
i know a guy whose father owns one
there's an occupation selling poetry to the masses
i wish i could find a mass maybe a mess would work better but i've never worked
so how could i know

well i know how you work
you work at fucking up
jerking off and fucking off
there's less lady in you
than in that gap-toothed greaser strolling by
his brains wrapped in felt
he feels up his childproof lighter

or maybe they're just smarter than you or me
and better at recognizing their face in the puddle
and when i say harvard cocksucker in cyberspace
you can be sure an american'll be there to tell me off

betty it was a lot easier in your day you had it tough
reporting to the anthropologist what everyone was wearing
it's wherever she wants to go she's the navigator
and later i'll give up son sleeping with men it's hard on the kids
who's daddy this week no i'm your uncle
tits touch tits and twat touches twat

if you spend time explicating lawn pizza and one-handed croquet
songs sung fastly have less charm than a reefer the size of my dick
it doesn't look too big till you get it in your mouth
then oh boy look out press down with your lips i don't need that harrassment

if you could take me around this country and explain it i'd appreciate it
i understand why we should look at trees and not people i'll pass the word
yucca leaves and yucka flux are more fun with yakuza jukes
junkerheads are now at the bottom of society on the street not the serfs
and i resent people who make more money than i do
no you get a job and i'll keep whining

let's end with a narrative, a good one if you can find one
oh right
catholic taste is out cathode art is in
i'm not in but i have one

later i'll marry someone rich that seems to be a good path to success
oh right
how about identity capitalism find a niche then another one then a third one
this is about selling books after all
don't get all romantic
did you enjoy this poem
what kind of runners are you wearing

MAN

rediscover at the rendezvous's faux legless women signs James Garner move a horse
around a TV antenna read the letters of General Stonewall Jackson at the stockmen's hotel with the gay bald guy playing an american womanizer the neon sign is 'broken' vote for your favourite neo-beatnik poet so the cowboy's hat is fixed in 2 bright positions their red faces squalling after sliding down the the fake man still glistening from his rough passage down the narrow channel of life he regarded me with a laviciously lugubrious expression okay kid take a deep breath and milk it back I commanded in mock military tone

one of favourite television programs is M*A*S*H, the seriocomic story of a fictional Army medical unit on the Korean War front never see a M*A*S*H segment without recalling my 'medical' career

not a career a job mucus streaming freely from his nose eyes etc he has two right hands, two hats what are you going to do your free gas and irregularity has been paid for hardee har har ah american sandwich chain ads bertolucci's desert contact lenses as if rectangular his name sounded like gallup

he's an old man not the rockford of the 70s, snappy, now he has a thick belt and she's 33 years old and living like a nun! sob-sister

hospitals are full of profit and centres for setting off biological clock, surrounded by sage,

families as awkward as they are on TV

george filgate territory, donald dransfield, guys in high school in the 70s in
northern alberta with slicked hair, unfashionable GWG jeans romanticize the
interior served up reflex quick fucking hick

hicksville territory to the max a three pick-up wedding, help written in paper
flowers on the tailgate, his jacket already off, going to finish his grade 12 &
only marginals walk around, kids, old, poor, native, realistic looking wounds
help for who bad acting grey gorilla hard to tell if it's not a commercial for
liferafts

Hey my kid made a picture of a gorilla from a CD-ROM! fucking fridge gallery

yes gorillas appreciate natural beauty just like humans as they emerge from
orange tube tents

luckily the gorilla's almost human, can talk with the help of a grey backpack
for fuselage bonding

quick take it off so she can rejoin the others – phew human technology isn't so
intrusive after all, but sitcom soap opera sweat they walk through a greenhouse
surrounded by people in fake fur and get the headache 2 partners left last night
why didn't they take me

mutt meryl streep wannabe is no john wayne and the k.s. mine looks
like a disney hotel

how to stop the vulgarization of a yuppie theme park you love – bring 'em in
museum wallpaper

Marky Mark's underwear line instigates rampant fucking: her father has a computer and glasses so we're sure of his class and shoulders remember when everyone was ethnic? Let's kick her ass read as harrassment not a snipped link in the sinning chain, honk if you love private prisons and public poverty. Sane shining take all those flying foam rubber cocks what use are they abs filled with discarded tits and cunts nowhere where can you buy an as-well-stocked sex shop don't think so no let's tighten our scrotums and get the job done stick that finger up his ass and ask for a raise again for the discerning consumer of hangnails cancel the gunsel let's say poetry's for fags and homos what does that say about foot fetishists reverse pedophilia wrinkle stilt skin

make moron poor encaustic panting harris mean
an english canadian accent not a canadian accent

access or pit one against the bother tillicum
maul maker marquee to rhyme with tardy

cantilevered: bottomy out heterosexuals she's heavier than she
tho neither has hair pour cement harrassment her
rasta cement cake over the pie or case nor shower shaved knorr

soupçon come and lick it split eager beavers for grants
and end up – where? – in libraries and classrooms?

or corpulent tailor-made whines, bureaucratic sellout
can't even focus on the grime on the window
let alone that looks beg and but one above buildings

a child crisis took her for everything she was worth
single mothers fly to close the flame of the fella's

what are we talking about here?

from lens to slot her dyke, a formidable opponent one the less
mackerel raincoated cartoons boxes teach with guards at your side
see if icarus blew it bigtime chez vous pal
hobnob with the best brass it makes no nevermind fucking burton
view palmoil celled lexuses and who wants a window with no holes
comparisons with no compo fallacies to better your lies without
slipping the syllable shift with a capital allowance cherchez l'argent
keep the stacked tyranny captain submarine cultures smell like stacked meat
let's say it worked & you were alive to see it work it was working already was
the problem making it work & if it works better less then what no name notoriety
can it go that big that way

& stay the different

safety break
            not debarked lumber

puke in each other's mouth as a recycling gesture

rock on kamloops on rock on kamloops ice machine on
the sugar snow satellite dishes rock on mickey swimming pools
sgt. flaherty's chevrons cold desert loud organic arid facing view
tacky motels track golf carts as work vehicles rich acres
not like owning a corner downtown feet in the air
but newly landed looking out & owning the view master
truck wedding help in flowers on the gate what are
we talking about here she bolts no stiffeners required pay
a ransom to have a family again throw a skull
cracker at that sucker orange peel bucket a hard squash

the tenor scrape of a lid on an empty grave
a hole in a flag suddenly term spirit gulag sells
former holidays bitter we're hoping for an angel tree
aging stalag insist the crime video shows her tan fringed
flatwear rug berm i love to see the sailors when
they're not there sewing mammal syllogism fucked internet patches before
puberty a wetter sweater damn kids & their j-pop knowledge
give 'me the boot but he doesn't know industrial health
& safety regs a new opium pipe of deer bare
a feather end hairdo bung up on the flying farm

a caul ritual on the ledge of the bash barely
edge of the bush a used car lot in labrador
a cross unknown volkswagens float stick brand sticks as
lined and signed hockey stick blades like incense holders ball
signed Dave hockey stuffed in his mouth a with the
dyke punk novel drunken nights around Clue those who find
the bodies death is suicide for i miss you a
lot every you, it's so shitty down here i wish
i could be up there with dad sewed up my
womb tight my baby's bleeding down my mouth from the

lawn of polished resin skulls t-shirt rake up those eyeballs
off an invisible goat's rains down the muck mucous red
hail and hitler's shitty sister what is writing to someone
whose dead father – what's the difference talking like a
dentist or continually christening stop just put that rug in
your own mouth wear blue jeans paul satire the dust
pan on the carpet orange gaping 'moon' put down julie's
d burrow's vincent's a tepid coffee drool moves buy an
american tree for cheaper library owner pisses on us free
skating and a lacking screws in there the slapshot or

blades emblazoned with fibreglass tape honey hockey stick stink 'some
narration' ruptured black the same in spanglish sometimes pro's hurt
or for short story rat man or your rat mom
leave you would you rather leave your miles landing death
landing death by committee resistance is futile to the collective
to a naval post with smug potatoes as if they
were handcuffed your own beeswax

At this juncture it may be as well to tell you that I did not exactly hit it off with the intellectuals in Toronto, and I suppose that it is too much to expect that intellectuals from more clement regions (more clement towards the Intelligence) should be welcomed ...

— Wyndham Lewis to Lorne Pierce, 17 June 1941

Some of these poems have appeared in *Canadian Literature*, *Sulfur* and *Torque*.
'Feminist Trilogy' was privately printed in 1997

Typeset in Matrix and printed at the Coach House Press on bpNichol Lane
Edited by Victor Coleman
Cover art by Phil McCrum

To read the online version of this text and other titles from Coach House Books, visit our website: www.chbooks.com

To add your name to our e-mailing list, write: mail@chbooks.com

Toll free: 1 800 376 6360

Coach House Books
401 Huron Street (rear) on bpNichol Lane
Toronto, Ontario
M5S 2G5